Did you hear Oral Roberts died?

One of the checks bounced.

What do Michael Jackson and the Red Sox first baseman have in common?

They both wear gloves for nothing.

Why was the Polish athlete thrown off the Olympic team?

They found traces of Pepsi in his urine.

Why is Halley's comet so frustrated?

It only comes once every seventy-six years.

What's the difference between Howdy Doody and President Reagan?

You can't see Reagan's strings.

Books by Maude Thickett

Outrageously Offensive Jokes I
Outrageously Offensive Jokes II
Outrageously Offensive Jokes III
Outrageously Offensive Jokes IV

Published by POCKET BOOKS

Most Pocket Books are available at special quantity discounts for bulk purchases for sales promotions, premiums or fund raising. Special books or book excerpts can also be created to fit specific needs.

For details write the office of the Vice President of Special Markets, Pocket Books, 1230 Avenue of the Americas, New York, New York 10020.

Outrageously

OFFENSIVE JOKES IV

MAUDE THICKETT

PUBLISHED BY POCKET BOOKS NEW YORK

This joke book may offend. That's why we call it *Outrageously Offensive Jokes*. The jokes included in this work are products of the author's imagination and fancy. No statements made about any person, product or place in any of these jokes should be taken as true.

Another *Original* publication of POCKET BOOKS

POCKET BOOKS, a division of Simon & Schuster, Inc.
1230 Avenue of the Americas, New York, N.Y. 10020

ISBN: 0-671-64908-6

First Pocket Books printing November 1987

10 9 8 7 6 5 4 3 2 1

POCKET and colophon are trademarks of
Simon & Schuster, Inc.

Printed in the U.S.A.

For Robin, Baby Gary, Fred, Jackie, Rob, and my hero Howard Stern, defender of our constitutional right of freedom of speech and whose morning mania is better than coffee and sometimes sex . . .

Acknowledgments

Special thanks to the gang in Pocket Sales, Vinny V., Dennis E., Mr. Tony, Moskey, Blob, Ronda K., my friends in Telephone Sales. Also thanks to Joe and Rose C., Russel and Cindy B., and K.B. with a T. Also Valentine, Aja, Wags, and Petey. And to Les, A. and Jay "who wanted a calendar."

Contents

Celebrities

What are N, O, and P?

Mary Beth Whitehead's next three kids.

◆

Why did Alpo hire Lorne Greene to do commercials?

They found him lying in his office licking his balls.

◆

What do you call a crooning cartoon character who ricochets off walls?

Sheriff Bing Bing Bing Crosby.

◆

How did the newspaper report the death of the founder of Kentucky Fried Chicken?

Colonel Sanders Kicks the Bucket.

◆

What do you get when you put 1,000 monkeys in front of 1,000 typewriters?

The staff of the *New York Post*.

♦

What movie stars Diane Keaton in search of well-hung mechanics?

Looking for Mr. Goodwrench.

♦

Why did Maria Shriver marry Arnold Schwarzenegger?

Because they are trying to breed bullet-proof Kennedys.

♦

What do you get when you cross a Japanese artist with a dead fat Broadway actor?

Yoko Coco.

♦

Did you hear about the new video game called Don King Kong?

Two gorillas fight each other while Don and the white woman wait in the limo.

What do you call the wife of a dead president who lays in the desert waiting to suck off Arabs?

Jackie Oasis.

A television producer was excitedly pitching an idea for a TV special to the network executive.

"I got Bernstein to compose the music."

"Leonard?"

"No, Joey Bernstein. Bright kid from UCLA. He's written a couple of jingles. Then for director, I got Coppola."

"Francis Ford?"

"No, Ernie Coppola. He's young, but you'll like him. And for the singer, I got Goulet."

"Robert?"

"Yeah."

"Shit."

How does Marlin Perkins keep tabs on his wife?

He has her tagged and banded, and implants a small radio transmitter in her left buttock.

◆

What do you call a sensitive actress?

Clitoris Leachman.

◆

What do Lucy's husband and a truss have in common?

They are both Ball holders.

◆

What do Michael Jackson and the Red Sox first baseman have in common?

They both wear gloves for nothing.

Why was Pia Zadora a bust in her role as Anne Frank?

Because every time it got to the part where the Germans break into the house, the audience would stand up and scream "She's in the fucking attic!"

◆

What do you get when you cross an artist with a really rude person?

Vincent Van Go Fuck Yourself.

◆

Did you hear that Imelda Marcos was a miner?

"That's mine and that's mine . . ."

◆

What do you call a guy who slightly resembles an actor who played James Bond?

Roger Moore or less.

◆

What's the difference between Joan Rivers and Johnny Wad?

He shaves, but her dick is bigger.

◆

What do you call the movie starring Arnold Schwarzenegger killing mice?

The Ex-Terminator.

◆

If Mary Beth Whitehead had twins, what would they be called?

M&M's.

◆

What do you call an acting family in a bathtub full of melted cheese?

Henry, Peter, and Jane Fondue.

◆

What do Len Bias and Rock Hudson have in common?

They both got some bad crack.

◆

What do they call Richard Pryor in Hollywood?

The toast of the town.

◆

Name a rock star that heels, rolls over, and plays dead.

Joe Cocker Spaniel.

◆

What's brown and floats in the dressing room bathroom of *The King and I*?

Yule Logs.

◆

What do you call the small penis of the slob on "The Odd Couple"?

Oscar's Minor Weiner.

◆

How do you know Popeye grew up on a potato farm?

He said, "I yam what I yam."

◆

What did the Mayberry newspaper headlines say when the deputy's spouse committed suicide by stabbing?

"Wife of Fife takes life with knife."

◆

What do you call Einstein masturbating?

A stroke of genius.

◆

What do you call Prince Rainier's deceased wife in Monaco?

Dis-Grace.

◆

How do you know Grace Kelly was really loose?

Because she was picked up more times than a princess phone.

◆

What has four wheels, an engine, and drives Sophia Loren into the mattress every night?

Carlo Pontiac.

◆

What do you call Barbra Streisand's pubic hair?

Yentl floss.

◆

What were Dennis Wilson's last three words?

Help me, Rhonda.

◆

Where would you find Prince Charles screwing pigs?

In Fucking-ham Palace.

◆

What do you call the editor of *Cosmopolitan* who goes "Nyuk, nyuk, nyuk"?

Helen Curly Brown.

◆

What game show stars Monty Hall fucking a pig?

"Let's Make a Squeal."

◆

What show stars Ted Danson and Shelley Long in a gay bar?

"Rears."

◆

What do you call an old moldy mystery writer?

Agatha Crusty.

Sports

What do Dwight Gooden and Julie Nixon Eisenhower have in common?

They both blow a little dope.

◆

What's black on the outside and white on the inside?

Len Bias's nose.

◆

Why did the Mets trade Dwight Gooden to the Chicago Bears?

Because they wanted a coke machine next to the Refrigerator.

◆

What do flowers and Len Bias have in common?

They both die two days after they've been picked.

◆

What do the New York Knicks and an ugly pimple-faced kid have in common?

It's almost impossible for either to score.

◆

What division is Len Bias playing on now?

Six foot and under.

◆

What's big, black, fat, and frozen?

Refrigerated Perry.

◆

Why did Dwight Gooden give up so many walks last year?

He liked freebasing.

◆

What cost Dwight Gooden $5,000, but had one calorie?

Diet coke.

◆

How do you know Darryl Strawberry's wife is a righty?

He can't hit lefties.

◆

Why did the battered wife decide to live with the New York Knicks?

They don't beat anybody.

◆

Why was the Polish athlete thrown off the Olympic team?

They found traces of Pepsi in his urine.

◆

Why didn't the Mets play last night?

Because Dwight Gooden snorted the line-up.

◆

Where does Walt Garrison's wife put her hygiene spray?

Between her cheek and gum.

◆

What's the difference between a fastball and a speedball?

Gooden had control of the fastball.

◆

How did Dwight Gooden spend $2,000 on lunch?

Ham and cheese with coke.

◆

Why did Dwight Gooden call the NAACP?

Because it stands for Never Admit Any Cocaine Problem.

◆

What's white, fluffy, costs $5,000, and sits on the mound?

Dwight Gooden's rosin bag.

◆

Why was the gay boxing match so exciting?

It was fifteen rounds of exchanging blows.

◆

What has ten legs, one big ball, and is black?

A starting five.

◆

What's Dwight Gooden's new position?

Snortstop.

◆

What do you call coffee made from athletes' underwear?

Jock full of nuts.

Black

What does a black man call his ideal woman?

Gorilla my dreams.

◆

How do you play poker in Howard Beach?

Two clubs beats three spades.

◆

How does the Ku Klux Klan go surfing with Negroes?

They hang ten.

◆

What do you call a black girl's vaginal crust?

Velveeta's cheese.

◆

Why did the white man bring blacks to America?

Because the Indians weren't good joke material.

◆

What did the police artist sketch when a woman described the man who raped her as being blond-haired, blue-eyed, and well-dressed?

A nigger.

◆

What does the lady say when she sees the picture?

That's him.

◆

What do you call blacks who read *Lord of the Rings*?

Tolkien Negroes.

◆

How do you know Davy Crockett was a racist?

He wore coon-skin caps.

◆

What is the opening line of the Black Theatre production of *Hamlet*?

"To be, or not to be, that be the question."

◆

What do you call an Ethiopian woman with a vaginal infection?

A quarter-pounder with cheese.

◆

Why won't Jesse Jackson ever become president?

They don't make bullet-proof Monte Carlos.

◆

What is the biggest fear of any married black man?

That his wife will evolve and he won't.

◆

What do you call a black in college?

Janitor.

◆

What does a bigot call it when a black is hung on a tree branch?

The jig is up.

◆

What do blacks call a modern-day plantation owner?

Warden.

◆

What do you call a law firm that has a bread company, a Jew, and a black for partners?

Arnold, Schwartz, and Nigger.

◆

What do you call a black woman in a stately home?

Maid.

◆

What do you call an African playwright?

William Shakes-spear.

◆

What do they call a dead baby born in the morning in Ethiopia?

Good eating.

◆

What do you call a black slave who disgraces her family?

A cotton-pickin' shame.

◆

What did the dumb black guy do after he won the lottery?

He bought a limo, then hired a white guy to sit in the back.

◆

A lost Japanese World War II soldier returned from the Philippine jungle after thirty-eight years. Upon arriving at his village, he learned that his wife was shacking up with a Negro and a Jew. Shocked, he asked her if it was true and she answered, "What motherfucker tell you that meshugenuh?"

◆

Did you hear about the new video game called Black-man?

Two nostrils chase after a line of coke.

◆

Why is it better to have nuclear power plants in your neighborhood instead of Negroes?

They are cleaner, more efficient, waste less energy, and don't leave cans of malt liquor in your yard.

◆

What do rednecks call the man who killed Martin Luther King?

James Earl Ray of Sunshine.

◆

What do you call a gay Ethiopian?

An African queen.

◆

What was the name of the black Secretary of the Interior?

James Say Watt.

Sex

What do you have when a famous movie monster stuffs his dick into your beer mug?

Frank in stein.

◆

What's the difference between exotic and psychotic?

Exotic is wearing a French tickler, psychotic is wearing French toast.

◆

Why were 1, 2, 3, 4, 5, and 6 scared?

Because 7 ate 9.

◆

How do you know your girlfriend is really hot?

When you put your hand in her panties and it feels like you're feeding a horse.

◆

Why didn't the cross-eyed seamstress ever get a period?

She couldn't mend straight.

◆

What do you call a soap opera starring testicles?

"Genital Hospital."

◆

If I had a rooster and you had a donkey and your donkey ate my rooster's feet, what would I have?

Two feet of my cock in your ass.

◆

What do you call the sweat on your body after you've screwed your own sister?

Relative humidity.

◆

What do you call Kermit fucking Miss Piggy?

A frog log in a hog.

◆

What do you call a bunch of men fucking mannequins?

Guys in dolls.

◆

A man walked into a diner and ordered a hamburger. The sweaty cook grabbed a patty of meat, placed it under his armpit, and repeatedly raised and lowered his arm to form a patty.

"That's disgusting," exclaimed the customer.

"Yeah? You should see how we make glazed doughnuts."

◆

What Dickens character liked to squeeze tits?

David Coppa-feel.

◆

47

Two male flies are flying over a cow pasture littered with shit. One of them spots a female fly sitting on a cow chip.

"Watch me make my move on the sweet-looking piece over there."

The male zips down to a neighboring turd and says in a suave voice, "Excuse me, honey, is this stool taken?"

◆

Did you hear about the old geezer who ate a whole bushel of oysters, but couldn't get a boner?

All was not lost; he shit three pearls the next day!

◆

What do you call blowing Dracula?

Going down for the Count.

◆

What do a midget and Johnny Wad have in common?

Both have dicks two inches from the floor.

On the eve of the Battle of Gettysburg, General Grant searched desperately for lodging for his weary troops. Having little luck, he dispatched Lieutenant Cox to check homes in one direction while he took the troops to a large mansion beyond the next hill. Grant knocked on the door of what turned out to be a large brothel. The general explained the situation to the madam.

"Well, how many are you?" asked the madam.

"A hundred men without Cox."

"You gotta be kidding."

What do you call a woman's vagina after she's been fucked by a well-hung Martian?

The Valley of the Green Giant.

Why is a defense contractor like a hooker?

They both charge $100 for a screw.

What do you call a Spanish whore who loves to give blow jobs?

A Señor-eater.

◆

How do you get a break in a porn movie?

The director says, "Take five inches."

◆

What do a man whacking his carrot and an expert fisherman have in common?

They are both master baiters.

◆

Why is Halley's comet so frustrated?

It only comes once every seventy-six years.

◆

Why is there such a high drop-out rate at proctology school?

The students just can't seem to take it in the end.

◆

What do you call an audience full of women clapping while having their period?

A standing ovulation.

◆

What do you call a big fat alien slob who fucks anybody?

Jabba the Slut.

◆

Why did the chef's penis hurt?

He learned to cook at the Sorbonne.

◆

What do hookers call money paid by midget customers?

Minimum wage.

◆

What's the most popular pick-up line at a NASA base bar?

Your pad or mine?

◆

Two Hell's Angels ran into each other on the street.
"Hey, where ya been lately?"
"I got married last month."
"No shit. How's the sex?"
"Not so good, but at least you don't gotta wait on line."

◆

What do you call a doctor who specializes in treating horny fat women's vaginas?

A rhinocologist.

◆

What do you call a gorgeous virgin with her period?

A bloody shame.

◆

When is Chinese food at its happiest?

When it's eaten out.

◆

Bumper sticker on a car: Bowlers have Big Balls.

◆

What other reason did Cinderella have for getting home by midnight?

Because at the stroke of twelve her diaphragm turned back into a trampoline.

◆

What do you call a group of twelve men with large pricks?

A hung jury.

◆

What do you call hookers waiting for boats to come in?

Portholes.

◆

What do you call vegetables that lick each other's vaginas?

Les-beans.

Why did the popular hooker dab scum behind her ears?

She wanted to maintain the sweet smell of success.

Why don't epileptics French-kiss?

They might swallow each other's tongues.

When is your hair happiest?

When it's blown dry.

What's the difference between a cowlick and a vaginal air burst?

One is a fussy part and the other a pussy fart.

Politics

What did Corazon Aquino say to the old regime as she kicked them out of the Philippines?

On your Marcos, set, go.

◆

What has eleven legs and lives in Cape Cod?

Ted Kennedy's family.

◆

What do you have when you take a '73 Chrysler, yesterday's pastry, and President Reagan?

An old Dart, an old tart, and an old fart.

◆

Why didn't Hitler wear rings?

Because he despised Jew-elry.

◆

What do they call an ex-president who likes to suck cock in Mexico?

El B.J.

◆

What's the difference between Howdy Doody and President Reagan?

You can't see Reagan's strings.

◆

What is Waldheimer's disease?

It's when you get old and forget that you were a Nazi.

◆

What do you call rich people pissing on you?

Reagan's trickle-down theory.

◆

How did the Speaker of the House introduce Gerald R. Ford?

And now, here's the latest dope from Washington.

◆

What Nazi leader had a hamster concentration camp?

Joseph Gerbils.

◆

What's German, has little factual data, and smells like shit?

Hitler's Diarrheas.

◆

What sound does Hitler make when he sneezes?

Aah-aah-aah-JEW!

◆

What do Democrats call farts?

Republican breathalyzer tests.

Religion

Why is pro wrestling like TV evangelists?

Because you know they are both fake, but you still find idiots who watch them.

Did you hear Oral Roberts died?

One of the checks bounced.

Define Miracle Whip.

What Jim Bakker does to his wife when he feels kinky.

Why was Tammy Bakker upset when she heard that her husband was fucking his secretary?

Because she ran out of liquor and pills.

What does Jim Bakker call a double orgasm?

The second coming.

◆

A rotten bastard passed away and realized he was on his way to Hell. As the doors opened, there before him was an enormous room filled with people standing in shit that came up to their necks. He walked cautiously over to the nearest person and asked, "Is this Hell?"

The person replied, "Yes."

He then blurted out, "Why, this isn't so bad."

Just then, Satan came over the intercom and said, "Okay, the coffee break for today is over. Everyone back on your heads."

◆

What does Tammy Bakker call a shot of whiskey?

A Bible belt.

◆

To pass the time on a long flight, Pope John Paul II was working on a crossword puzzle. He leaned over to the Archbishop and asked, "Begging your pardon, but what would be a four-letter word for *woman* that ends in U-N-T?"

"Why, that would be *aunt*," the Bishop replied.

The Pope then asked, "Do you have an eraser?"

◆

What do you call three turds in a Vatican bathroom?

Pope Poop the Third.

◆

Why don't Baptists fuck standing up?

They are afraid it might lead to dancing.

◆

What do you call a religious woman in a garbage bag?

Blue Nun.

◆

Who kills Christ and says, "Har, me matey"?

Pontius Pirate.

◆

International

What soup is the Russian favorite?

Mushroom.

◆

What do you call a whore in Spain who doesn't charge money?

A free-holey.

◆

Why was the Polack arrested for indecent exposure?

Someone asked him to count to eleven.

◆

Why are most Italians called "Tony"?

Because when they got to Ellis Island they stamped "TO N.Y." on their foreheads.

◆

What is the five-day weather forecast over Chernobyl?

Three days.

◆

Why don't Polish heroin users worry about getting AIDS from needles?

Because they wear rubbers.

◆

What's the difference between Iran and an armpit?

One can of deodorant will take care of the armpit.

◆

The Godfather calls Vito to come into his office.
"Vito, I want you to do something for me."
"Anything, Godfather. Just ask."
"I want you to take this cup and jerk off into it."

So Vito goes into the bathroom, and about three minutes later, comes back out and hands the cup to the Godfather.

"Vito, I want you to do me another favor."

"Anything for you, Godfather."

"I want you to take another cup and jerk off into it."

So Vito takes off for the bathroom again. About ten minutes later, he emerges with another cup and hands it to the Godfather.

"Vito, will you do me another favor?"

"Anything, Godfather, just name it."

"Will you take another cup and jerk off into it?"

"Anything for you, Godfather."

So Vito, tired and shaky at this point, heads off to the bathroom. About a half hour later, Vito comes out looking exhausted and haggard. He hands the cup to the Godfather.

"Vito, will you do me one more favor?"

"Anything, Godfather."

"Now you can take my daughter to the airport."

What do you call a Russian nerd?

A red square.

Why was the Polish child upset when the label fell off his red crayon?

How was he gonna know what color it was?

What do you call an Iranian who stops your car and takes your money?

Ayatollbooth Khomeini.

What do the Russians and a girl who likes to suck sailors' cocks have in common?

They both want the crew's missiles.

What list is one page long and all lies?

The Guineas' Book of World Records.

Why do Polish women cook without underwear?

To keep the flies off the food.

What's large, flat, burnt, and glows in the dark?

Lebanon, if Reagan had any balls.

◆

How does a Polack take his girl out for a royal evening?

Dinner at Burger King, dessert at Dairy Queen.

◆

What do you call the underground crime syndicate that fills vaginas with cement before dumping the body in the river?

The Muffia.

◆

What has feathers and glows?

Chicken Kiev.

◆

Where do Polish occultists live?

Hell-sinki.

◆

Why did the Pole keep getting so many parking tickets?

Because he stopped putting money in the meters when the gumballs didn't come out.

◆

What do you call a Hindu whore?

A snake charmer.

◆

Why are Russians in Chernobyl having more children?

So they can have a light in every room.

◆

Why were the Polish inmates caught while trying to escape?

They asked the guard to turn on the searchlight so they could see where they were going.

Why did the Polish tailor want to be a lawyer?

He figured the money must be great if they get million-dollar suits.

◆

What do they call a swinger in Moscow?

Hotski to Trotski.

◆

A Polack and an Italian are at a bar watching the eleven o'clock news. A woman on the news is threatening to jump.

The Italian says, "Fifty bucks, I say she jump."

The Polack says, "You're on."

The woman jumps.

The Italian says, "I'm not taking your money; I saw the six o'clock news."

The Polack says, "I did, too, but I never would have thought she'd do it again."

◆

Why do Polacks wear rubbers on their ears?

So they don't get hearing AIDS.

◆

What do you call a Spaniard who eats unleavened bread?

Man of La Matzo.

◆

A man walks into a bar and says to the bartender, "Hey, I've got a really funny Polish joke to tell ya!"

The bartender says: "Hey, listen. Ya see that guy over there? He's the chief of police and he's Polish. Ya see that guy over there? He's the bouncer. He's Polish too. And me, I'm Polish. So do you really want to tell that joke in here?"

The man hesitates and says, "Naw, then I'd have to explain three times!"

◆

What goes best with Chicken Kiev?

A Black Russian.

◆

Why did the Polack stop skeet shooting?

The damn things tasted terrible.

Gay

How do you know you're in a gay amusement park?

They pass out gerbils in the tunnel of love.

◆

Why was the gay embarrassed when he was caught blowing the well-hung black delivery boy?

Because he was caught with a foot in his mouth.

◆

What does a gay turkey say after he sucks your cock?

Gobble, gobble, gobble de goop.

◆

How many faggots does it take to screw in a light bulb?

One, as long as there's plenty of oil and he's real careful.

◆

What did the mother say to her midget artist son after she found out he had AIDS?

You are Too Loose Lautrec.

◆

How do you prevent homos from getting AIDS?

Tell 'em to sit down and keep their mouth shut.

◆

Why were the other vegetables worried for Sprout?

They found out the Jolly Green Giant was a member of NAMBLA.

◆

What painting do members of NAMBLA love?

Little boy blew.

◆

What weighs 250 pounds and swims in the San Francisco Bay?

Moby Dyke.

◆

Did you hear Vaseline is coming out with new labels for its petroleum jelly?

They're going to have a picture of missing gerbils on it.

◆

Why did the doctors give Liberace six more weeks to live?

The gerbil came out of his ass and saw his shadow.

◆

What did one gerbil say to the other when he saw the gay man swish into the pet store?

"Don't panic! Just turn your back and act like a dog."

◆

Bumper sticker: Liberace was great on the piano, but sucked on the organ.

♦

What's the difference between a warning on a package and a Liberace sex toy?

One is Handle With Care and the other is a candle with hair.

♦

What do you call the organization of men who sexually abuse young pigs?

HAMBLA.

♦

What did the blind gay say as he was eating out another's asshole?

I can't see shit.

♦

How do you know your little boy will grow up to be gay?

He plays Lick the Can.

◆

What does a gerbil call hemorrhoids?

Speed bumps.

◆

What did one gerbil say to the other?

Let's go to the local gay bar and get shit-faced.

◆

How did Liberace burn his ass?

He forgot to blow out the candle.

◆

What magic words did Liberace say before he made wax sticks disappear up his ass?

Candle-abra cadabra.

◆

How do homos take their eggs?

Up the ass, of course.

◆

What do you call a gay child with splinters in his ass?

Bat boy.

◆

Why did they bury Liberace upside down?

So his friends would recognize him.

◆

What do you call a detective show starring Liberace and Rock Hudson?

"Moonbiting."

◆

Where do most gays go in South America for vacation?

Crack-Ass, Venezuela.

◆

How did the Statue of Liberty get AIDS?

From the mouth of the Hudson.

◆

On what charges was Liberace brought up when they caught him cornholing a thief?

Aiding and abutting a criminal.

◆

What do you call a bunch of gays in a Nazi camp?

Hogan's homos.

◆

What do you call a musical about gay cowboys?

Okla-homo.

◆

What's the highest rank a homo can achieve in the navy?

Rear admiral.

◆

Why didn't the producers of *A Streetcar Named Desire* ask for Tennessee Williams's advice when they casted for all-new roles?

Because he's a dead homo.

◆

What does a gay look into when he dresses?

A rear-view mirror.

◆

What do you call it when one gay kills another?

Homo-cide.

◆

Why did the gay get a parking permit in the slums?

So he could use his asshole as an amusement park for rodents.

◆

What's the difference between Liberace and a closet homosexual?

Liberace can play the piano.

What Do You Call . . .

What do you call a guy who likes to stick his dick in gays' buns?

Frank.

◆

What do you call a flaccid penis on a faggot?

A limp shrimp on a wimp.

◆

What do you call a girl who loves to give blowjobs?

Hedy.

◆

What do you call a woman who likes to go down on other women?

Muffy.

◆

What do you call a guy who cancels laws?

Vito.

◆

What do you call a woman who lets frogs sit on her face?

Lily.

◆

What do you call a woman with a moist pussy?

Marsha.

◆

What do you call a woman during her period?

Flo.

◆

What do you call a cheap Jew's daughter?

Penny.

◆

What do you call a guy who has diamonds instead of testicles?

Jules.

◆

What do you call a guy who lets people shit all over him?

John.

◆

What do you call a guy with mucus in his throat?

Fleming.

◆

What do you call a guy with a steel cock?

Spike.

◆

What do you call a guy with a five-inch penis?

Norm.

◆

What do you call a girl who loves to blow?

Gale.

◆

What do you call a woman who lets men walk all over her?

Dolly.

◆

What do you call a dead girl washed up on the beach?

Shelley.

◆

What do you call a woman lost in New York?

Wanda.

◆

What do you call a girl who wets her bed?

Sissy.

◆

What do you call a woman who purrs when you fuck her?

Kitty.

◆

What do you call a guy who fucks animals?

Barney.

◆

What do you call a girl who farts all the time?

Fanny.

Jewish

What is a Jewish bird call?

Cheap, cheap, cheap.

◆

Who says "Mazel tov Bing Bing Bing!"?

Ricochet Rabbi.

◆

What do you call a group of racist Jews who toast bagels on people's front lawns?

The Klu Klux Kleins.

◆

Did you hear about the new Japanese Jewish restaurant?

So sue me.

◆

What do you call a big-nosed pancake-maker?

Aunt Jew-mima.

◆

What's the difference between a Jewish woman and an Italian woman?

Italian women have real orgasms and fake diamonds.

◆

When does it get really hot in a Jewish bedroom?

When the air conditioner breaks down.

◆

What did they call lynching Jews in Nazi Germany?

Soap on a rope.

◆

What's a wrench?

A place where Jewish people keep horses.

◆

What's Jewish, leads a nation, and has cream cheese all over him?

Menachem Bagel.

◆

What's the difference between a JAP and a toilet?

The toilet doesn't follow you around after you're done using it.

◆

What is the difference between a Jew and pizza pie?

A pizza doesn't scream when you put it in the oven.

◆

What do you call a bunch of kikes who pray to milk by-products?

Jews for Cheeses.

◆

What movie starred Michael Douglas, Kathleen Turner, and Irving Feldberg?

Jew of the Nile.

◆

How do Jewish women entertain?

With a little whine and cheese.

◆

What do you call purple Israelis?

Grape Jews.

◆

What do you call a cop show set in a Jewish neighborhood?

"Hillel Street Blues."

◆

What do you get when you cross a cartoon character with a Jew?

Hagar the Horriblewitz.

◆

What drink did Hitler make out of concentration camp victims' faces?

Mint Jew-lips.

◆

What month did Hitler hate?

Jew-ly.

◆

Why did Hitler hate kids?

Because they are all Jew-veniles.

◆

What literary character was a doctor who turned into a hideous Jewish monster?

Dr. Jekyll and Mr. Stein.

◆

Did you hear that a Jewish group bought Irving Trust?

They are calling it Trust Irving.

◆

What do you call a Jewish pirate?

Captain Schnook.

◆

What do you call a Jew sitting on a vegetable?

Cohen on the cob.

◆

Why did Hitler shove all the judges and lawyers in Germany into an oven?

He couldn't stand the Jew-dicial system.

◆

What position does a Jew play in football?

Nose guard.

◆

What do you call a Western about a stupid Jew?

"Gun-Schmuck."

◆

What color business suits did Jews wear in Nazi Germany?

Charcoal gray.

◆

What was Santa's answer after he was asked how he knows not to go into a Jewish home on Christmas Eve?

I can smell a kike a mile away.

◆

Miscellaneous

What don't you ask a woman drinking coffee at a mastectomy clinic?

"One lump or two?"

♦

What kids' cereal has little scrotums in it?

Cap'n Crotch.

♦

What's the difference between a Porsche and a porcupine?

A porcupine has pricks on the outside.

♦

When does a Puerto Rican become a Spaniard?

When he marries your daughter.

♦

What's the definition of a sensitive man?

A guy who doesn't make his girlfriend blow him after he butt-fucks her.

◆

What's the definition of busy?

One set of jumper cables at a Puerto Rican funeral.

◆

What do you call a mushroom that parties?

A fun-guy.

◆

What's the dirtiest thing ever said on TV?

"Ward, weren't you a little rough on the beaver last night?"

◆

A young boy is playing with his train set in the living room while his mother cooks. He lets the train go around the track ten times, stops it, and says, "All you bastards who wanna get in, get in. All you bastards who wanna get out, get out." He lets the train go around another ten times, stops it, and again says, "All you bastards wanna get in, get in. All you bastards wanna get out, get out."

With that, the mother comes storming into the living room and tells her son to go sit in the corner for one hour for speaking so filthily.

One hour goes by and the mother tells the little boy that he can go back and play with his trains again. The little boy sends the train around the track ten times, stops it, and says, "All you bastards wanna get in, get in. All you bastards wanna get out, get out. Anybody got a complaint about the delay, go see the bitch in the kitchen."

◆

What do you call a deer with no eyes?

No-eye deer.

◆

What do you call a deer with no eyes and no legs?

Still no-eye deer.

♦

What do you call a deer with no eyes, no legs, and no balls?

Still no fucking eye deer.

♦

What do you call Walt Disney's favorite dessert?

Mickey Mousse.

♦

What do you call a toy that pulls off Ken's testicles before throwing him in an oven?

A Klaus Barbie Doll.

♦

What is Helen Keller's favorite joke?

"What is a light bulb, and how do you screw it in?"

◆

What did the tired asshole say after a long shit?

I'm all pooped out.

◆

What famous murderer killed his victims with jellied meat?

Son of Spam.

◆

How does a teamster tell his son a bedtime story?

Once upon a time and a half ago . . .

◆

How do you know when your wife is a lousy cook?

She uses the smoke detector as a timer.

◆

Did you read the latest bathroom murder mystery?

The butler did it in his pants.

◆

What do you call four New Jersey kids on the floor of a car?

Exhausted.

◆

What do you call an Indian butler?

Mahat Macoat.

◆

What do you call a surgeon who hunts?

Dr. Kill-deer.

◆

Why did the network cancel the orchestra special?

Because there was already enough sax and violins on TV.

◆

What do you call a big oaf's testicle?

A lug nut.

◆

A woman walks into her therapist and says, "Doc, I'm so confused. One day I feel like a teepee, the next day, a wigwam. Teepee, wigwam, teepee, wigwam, teepee, wigwam . . ."

"*Stop!*" yells the therapist. "You're just too tense!"

◆

What's invisible and smells like worms?

A bird fart.

◆

What did the composer's wife say to the composer when she wanted to use a rectal thermometer?

Roll over, Beethoven.

◆

Why is a group of flesh-eaters like a jar of scrotum?

They're both Can-o-balls.

◆

What do you call the sweat of matadors?

Oil of Olé.

◆

What do a closed school and a woman who picks her nose and eats it have in common?

They both have no class.

◆

What do you call an hors d'oeuvre and the ugly woman you woke up with?

Pig in a blanket.

◆

What book did Darwin write that says all men came from shit?

The Origin of Feces.

◆

What do you call a female relative who rides the subways looking to shoot muggers and rapists?

A vigil-auntie.

◆

Why did the mommy vampire smack the bowl of tampons out of her son's hands?

No snacks between meals.

◆

What famous musical was about a family escaping from the Germans in an elevator?

The Sound of Muzak.

◆

Who said, "It used to be a white brick road, but I took care of it"?

Toto.

◆

What do you call a tailor's ass problem?

Hemmer-rhoids.

◆

What do you call an account where you save money to buy a testicle supporter?

A truss fund.

◆

What does a stud who lies tell you?

A cock and bull story.

◆

Why did the disgruntled French chef throw a grenade in the pastry tray?

He wanted to see Napoleon Blownapart.

◆

What music video station do Indians listen to?

M-Tee-Pee.

◆

What do you call an army officer who fucks everything up?

Major Disaster.

◆

What do you call an army officer who hits you for being bad?

Corporal Punishment.

◆

What do you call a well-hung groundskeeper?

The garden hose.

◆

What was found floating in the McDonald's bathroom?

McNuggets.

◆

Why was the man tired of having hemorrhoids?

Because he was the butt of every wisecrack.

◆

What do you call a circle of wagons, filled with
pudding, under Indian attack?

Custard's last stand.

◆

What do you call female army soldiers?

Puss in Boots.

◆

What's it called when two brothers shoot each
other?

Sibling riflery.

◆

What do you get when you cross a penis, a potato, and an ocean liner?

A dictatorship.

◆

Did you hear Anheuser-Busch merged with the Red Cross?

Their new slogan is "This Blood's for You."